W9-CNY-378

SCIENCE FICTION TO SCIENCE FACT

REPLICATORS

BY HOLLY DUHIG

50%

Gareth Stevens
PUBLISHING

Please visit our website, **www.garethstevens.com.**
For a free color catalog of all our high-quality books,
call toll free 1-800-542-2595 or fax 1-877-542-2596.

Cataloging-in-Publication Data

Names: Duhig, Holly.
Title: Replicators / Holly Duhig.
Description: New York : Gareth Stevens Publishing, 2018. | Series:
    Science fiction to science fact | Includes index.
Identifiers: ISBN 9781538214930 (pbk.) | ISBN 9781538213865
    (library bound) | ISBN 9781538214947 (6 pack)
Subjects: LCSH: Three-dimensional printing--Juvenile literature.
    | Nanotechnology -- Juvenile literature. | Technological
    innovations--Juvenile literature.
Classification: LCC TS171.95 D84 2018 | DDC 621.9'88--dc23

Published in 2018 by
Gareth Stevens Publishing
111 East 14th Street, Suite 349
New York, NY 10003

Copyright © 2018 BookLife

Written by: Holly Duhig
Edited by: John Wood
Designed by: Matt Rumbelow

Photo credits: Abbreviations: l-left, r-right, b-bottom, t-top, c-center,
m-middle. With thanks to Getty Images, Thinkstock Photo and iStockphoto.
Cover: bg – MaxyM; front – Halfpoint. 2 – Fer Gregory. 4 – Algol. 5 –
Luadthong. 6 – lassedesignen. 7: t1 – vs148; t2 – ESB Professional. 8: t –
Rick Partington; b – Vadim Sadovski. 9: t – Esteban De Armas; b – Raymond
Cassel. 10: l – Scanrail1; c – MrGarry. 11: t – BalancePhoto; b – tchara. 12:
t – dezignor; b – Aumm graphixphoto. 13: t – 123dartist; b – Andrii Zhezhera.
14 – Mix-space. 15: t – Yury Zap; b – doomu. 16 – Fer Gregory. 17 – Sylverarts
Vectors. 18 – CLUSTERX. 19 – Igor Zh. 20: t – Fotografiche; b – Joshua Jo.
21 – Robert Kneschke. 22: t – Roman3dAr; b – exopixel. 23 – Marcos Mesa
Sam Wordley. 24: bl – solarseven; tr – Stepan Kapl. 25: tr – eurobanks, br –
SNP_SS. 26: bg – Fer Gregory; br – ValIza. 27: Algo. 28: tr – Quality Master; br
Kate Artyukhova. 29: bg – acharyahargreaves; front – Albert Ziganshin. 30:
bg – camilkuo; br – racorn.

Printed in China
CPSIA compliance information: Batch CS18GS: For further information contact
Gareth Stevens, New York, New York at 1-800-542-2595.

SYSTEM
PROTECTION

3.52

1.41

CONTENTS

Words that appear like this can be found in the glossary on page 31.

REPLICATORS: THE FANTASY

HUNGRY?

If you could have anything to eat right now, what would it be? Spaghetti? Steak? Wouldn't it be great if there was a machine that could instantly make any food you wanted at the press of a button? Well I've got some news for you. Machines like this exist and here you can learn all about them.

In science fiction, these machines are called replicators because they **replicate** things from the real world and create them from nothing. You would just need to scan a single chocolate cake recipe, and the machine would know how to make chocolate cake copies forever. The more recipes you scan in, the more things the machine would know how to make. Imagine the possibilities! You could make copies of anything, like… double chocolate cake!

CREATING AND RECYCLING

Sorry, but we need to stop thinking about cakes for now. Replicators in science fiction are used to make other things too, such as tools, uniforms, and spare parts. They are sometimes even used to create air for people to breathe when they are in a spacecraft far away from Earth. Replicators are also able to destroy and recycle objects, like in Star Trek.

SOMETHING FROM NOTHING

One of the best things about a replicator is that it can create something out of thin air. But is this really possible? Well, it depends what you mean by "thin air." If you wanted to make a cake, you would need eggs, flour, butter, and all the rest of the ingredients. But what if you could make it from different ingredients, like a small amount of powder, or a large amount of energy? This is what we need to find out: what ingredients does a real replicator need, and what exactly could it make?

USES FOR REPLICATORS

FOOD

Replicators could help people in many, many ways. Think of all the problems we could solve if we could instantly create anything we wanted. We could make sure that everyone in the world had plenty of food, and no one would ever have to starve. We also wouldn't have to keep so many animals on farms, which would be better for the environment.

EVERYTHING BUT FOOD

However, it is not all about food. Replicators could be used to create things like furniture, books, or toys. Think how useful a replicator would be for a spacecraft far away in space with a broken engine! If the people onboard had a replicator that could create the engine part they needed, they could fix it right there.

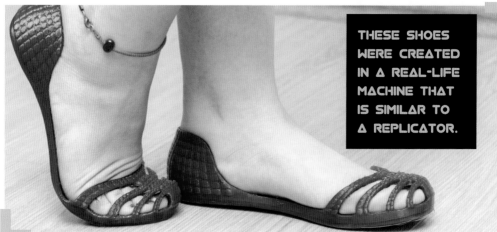

THESE SHOES WERE CREATED IN A REAL-LIFE MACHINE THAT IS SIMILAR TO A REPLICATOR.

LIVING TISSUE

Replicators would also be useful if you wanted to make living tissue. Replicators could make organs, such as hearts and lungs, for people who are sick. People who need organs usually have to wait a long time for one to be donated, but that wouldn't be the case if we had replicators. Think of all the lives it would save!

HOUSES

If you built a big enough replicator, there is no reason why you couldn't make an entire house! Using machines instead of people to build houses would be much quicker and would help people who become homeless in natural disasters. It would also help astronauts to set up bases on other planets in the future.

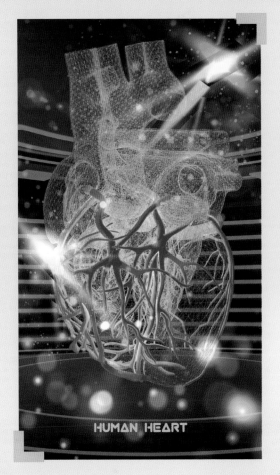

HUMAN HEART

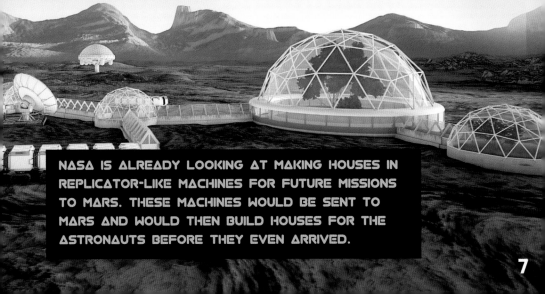

NASA IS ALREADY LOOKING AT MAKING HOUSES IN REPLICATOR-LIKE MACHINES FOR FUTURE MISSIONS TO MARS. THESE MACHINES WOULD BE SENT TO MARS AND WOULD THEN BUILD HOUSES FOR THE ASTRONAUTS BEFORE THEY EVEN ARRIVED.

REPLICATORS: THE REALITY

OK, let's stop talking about what we might do and talk about what we are doing. Can we replicate objects from nothing right now?

FOOD REPLICATORS

Right now we have devices that certainly look like the replicators of the future. By putting a small pod of ingredients in a machine and pressing a button, you could have a fully cooked meal in about 30 seconds.

It works by combining frozen, dried ingredients from the pod with different kinds of liquid stored inside the machine. It then cooks the meal extremely quickly.

As futuristic as that sounds, it's not the same as the replicators of science fiction. We still need to put ingredients in and replace the liquids when they run out. And the food replicators we have right now can only make a few meals. There's no double chocolate cake on the menu, so let's move on to some interesting things NASA is working on...

DESKTOP 3D PRINTER

NASA'S INTERESTING THINGS

NASA, America's space agency, has funded the design of a machine that will be able to create pizza for astronauts in space. Admittedly, these won't appear out of nowhere in a puff of smoke. They will use organic powders that are made from all sorts of things, including grass, insects, and algae. And it's not just about pizza. They want to design all sorts of replicator-like machines for people to use in space.

ONE DAY, ASTRONAUTS WILL GET THE PIZZA THEY DESERVE.

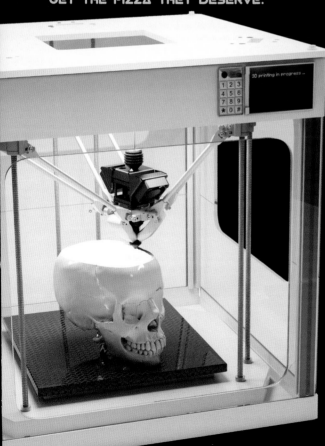

However, this is nothing new. NASA is just building on technology called 3-D printing. 3-D printing is probably the closest thing we've got to replicators in the present day, and they are getting better every day.

3-D PRINTING HAS BEEN AROUND SINCE THE 1980S. LOTS OF PEOPLE THINK IT IS GOING TO HAVE A BIG IMPACT ON THE WAY WE MAKE THINGS IN THE FUTURE.

HOW DOES 3-D PRINTING WORK?

When a normal printer puts words and images on a piece of paper, it is actually firing a layer of ink over the surface of the paper. The idea behind 3-D printers is to build up lots and lots of layers and create a 3-D object. Of course, 3-D printers use all sorts of different materials to build these layers, depending on what the object is going to be made from.

3-D printers can build objects from materials such as plastic, glass, metal, or even chocolate. The materials are usually in a powdered or liquid form and are often fused together by a laser or a type of glue. Once one layer is done, the machine will begin on the next layer, and then the next, until the entire object – whatever it may be – is finished.

3-D PRINTER BUILDING LAYERS

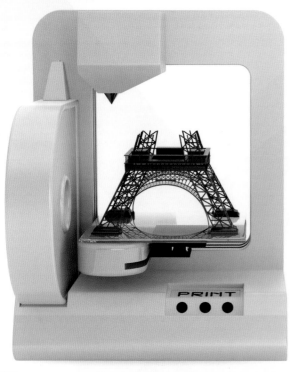

METAL CAN BE TURNED INTO A POWDER, WHICH CAN BE USED TO 3-D PRINT METAL OBJECTS.

MACHINES NEED A PLAN

Much like replicators in science fiction, 3-D printers need a plan for the objects they make. These act as a set of instructions for the printer, telling it how each layer should look. Most of the time, these plans are made on a computer and then sent to the printer.

3-D SCANNING

Sometimes these plans are made by scanning a real-life object with a special camera. The camera translates the object into a design that the computer can understand. The computer then splits up the design into layers and sends information about which materials are needed to make each layer to the printer. Then the fun begins!

AN OBJECT IS SCANNED INTO A COMPUTER.

WHAT CAN BE 3-D PRINTED?

NASA'S WRENCH

There is a 3-D printer on the International Space Station. Getting a 3-D printer to work in space is quite difficult because everything floats about in the air. But the world is full of clever people, and some of them managed to invent a printer that worked in the space station.

To test this printer, engineers on Earth designed a wrench and sent those designs to the 3-D printer on the International Space Station. The astronauts in space were then able to print the wrench and use it right away.

THE 3-D PRINTED WRENCH

CHOCOLATE

Fortunately, chocolate is a really good material to 3-D print with. To do this, you first have to melt the chocolate, and then you can squeeze it out into layers. As the layers cool and become solid, new layers can be built on top. This all sounds easy enough, right? Maybe the hardest part would be not eating the melted chocolate before it goes in the machine. Let's be honest, nobody can resist melted chocolate.

ONE IN EVERY HOME

One day, we may all have a 3-D printer in our homes. If this happens, it would be easy to replace anything that was old or broken. Did you knock your mom's vase of flowers on the floor? Quick, to the 3-D printer!

PRINTING SOMETHING LIKE A VASE COULD TAKE HOURS. LET'S HOPE NOBODY NOTICES IN THE MEANTIME.

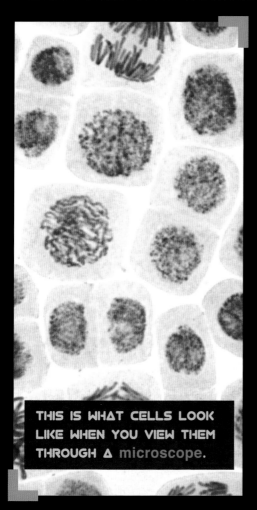

THIS IS WHAT CELLS LOOK LIKE WHEN YOU VIEW THEM THROUGH A microscope.

LIVING TISSUE

But maybe you are bored of plastics and metals. Maybe it's time to talk about something really weird – what about printing real body parts? Before we get onto this, we need to learn about cells. Every living thing is made out of cells. Animals, like cats, dogs, and even humans, are all made up of lots of different types of cells, each of which are good at different things. Complex combinations of these cells make up living tissue. Because of this, printing living tissue is going to be difficult – you can't just glue a load of cells together!

BIOPRINTING

3-D printers are capable of printing living tissue right now. However, if you want to see a beating heart popping straight out of a replicating machine, you might have to wait a while. Although nobody has been able to replicate a fully functioning organ for humans just yet, we are able to use 3-D printing to repair parts of organs, skin, and bone.

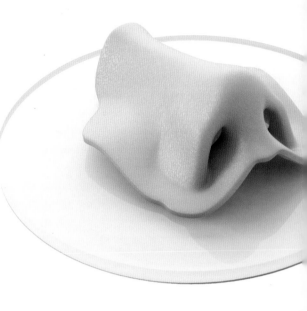

BIO-INKS

3-D printers usually use something called bio-ink to create living tissue. Bio-ink is a mixture of different cells and a **scaffold** which holds it all together in the right shape. To create the bio-ink, the printer usually has at least two **nozzles** – one printing cells and one printing the scaffold. After printing, the cells fuse together to create the tissue. The scaffold is often made out of a water-based **gel**, which is eventually washed away.

Not only is bioprinting useful for repairing living tissue, it can also be used to help fight diseases. By infecting 3-D printed tissue with a certain disease, scientists can then learn a lot about how that disease works. This is a safe way to study diseases because nobody gets sick.

GROWING MEAT IN LABORATORIES

Let's talk about food again. The ability to create living tissue means that we are now able to replicate meat to eat as food. The first step is to take cells from the animal you want to eat – for example, a cow. Now you need to feed the cells **nutrients** so that they will multiply until you have millions of other cells.

COWS DON'T MIND TOO MUCH IF YOU BORROW SOME OF THEIR CELLS. AFTER ALL, THEY HAVE TRILLIONS OF THEM.

These cells will naturally clump together and turn into strips of muscle. These strips are then mixed with fat and layered together using 3-D bioprinting. At the end of all that, you have meat for your burger! One day soon, you might have the chance to eat meat made in a laboratory. Maybe in the distant future, you will even be able to print your own steaks.

STEM CELLS: NATURE'S REPLICATORS

As you may have noticed, cells are like nature's replicators. These cells seem to be very good at copying themselves. But unlike 3-D printers, most cells can't multiply into anything they want. The cells that make up your skin can only make other skin cells and the cells that make up your bones can only make more bone cells. However, there is a special kind of cell that does things a bit differently.

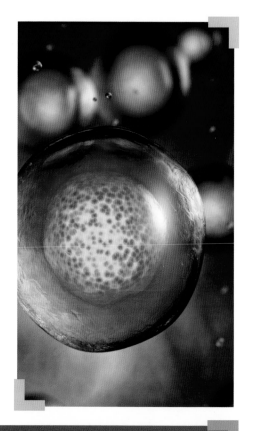

These special cells are called stem cells, and they are nature's greatest replicator. Stem cells are special because they can turn into lots of different cells. When a mother is pregnant, a bunch of stem cells are formed inside of her body. This is called an embryo. The embryo's stem cells divide and multiply to make a baby. A whole baby! All its fingers, organs, eyes, and skin are made from the stem cells that are cared for inside the mother's body.

STEM CELLS EXIST IN ADULTS AND CHILDREN TOO. WHILE THEY CAN'T TURN INTO EVERY KIND OF CELL, THEY ARE STILL VERY USEFUL IN REPAIRING OUR BODIES.

STEM CELL RESEARCH

Scientists around the world are working hard to fully understand stem cells. These special cells could be very useful in treating illnesses and repairing damage to the body. For example, Parkinson's disease is an illness which causes certain cells in the brain to be destroyed. Unlike other cells, some brain cells don't replace themselves naturally. This causes all sorts of problems in the brain. For example, it can often make a person with Parkinson's shake and move rigidly and slowly. But by injecting stem cells into the brain, we may be able to replace the dead cells and repair the damage. Scientists aren't sure yet, which is why lots of research has to be done on stem cells.

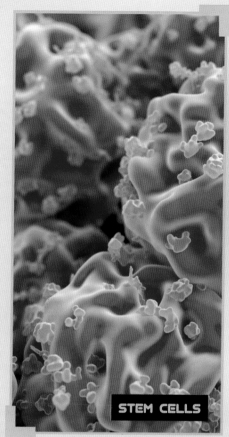

STEM CELLS

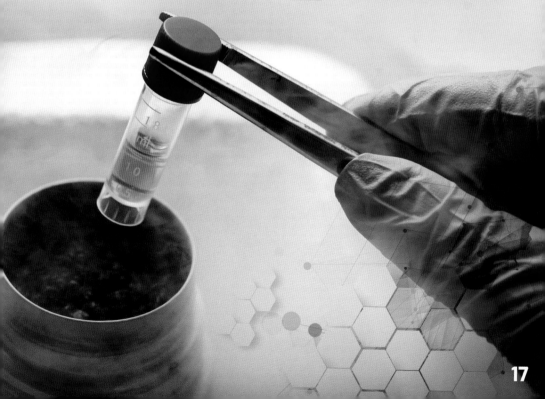

CLONING

If you could scan yourself into a 3-D bioprinter, would you? Would you press print, and cause an exact copy of yourself to come out? Well, it turns out that this is something scientists have been looking at quite a while. When you make a copy of an animal or plant, it is called cloning. However, we couldn't clone you using 3-D printing. We don't have cameras that can scan things as small as cells – at least, not yet. You are far too complex to clone using a 3-D printer. But scientists have cloned animals before. To do this, they used a method called nuclear transferring. First, let's brush up on some science before we look at what nuclear transferring is.

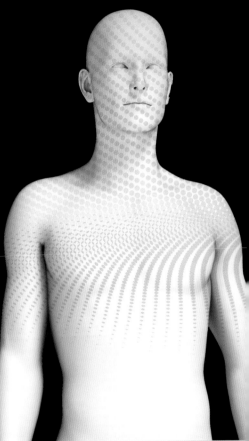

THE NUCLEUS

The cells that make up plants and animals all have a few things in common. One thing they have in common is that they all have a nucleus. This is the control center for the cell – it tells the cell how to grow and how to multiply. It is a bit like the cell's brain. The nucleus also stores the DNA. DNA is very important if you want to clone something, so we'd better take a closer look at it.

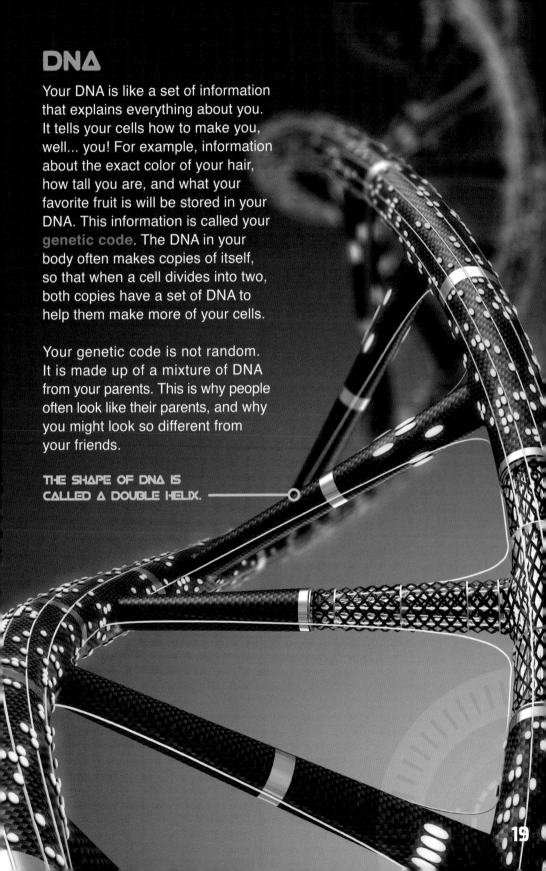

DNA

Your DNA is like a set of information that explains everything about you. It tells your cells how to make you, well... you! For example, information about the exact color of your hair, how tall you are, and what your favorite fruit is will be stored in your DNA. This information is called your genetic code. The DNA in your body often makes copies of itself, so that when a cell divides into two, both copies have a set of DNA to help them make more of your cells.

Your genetic code is not random. It is made up of a mixture of DNA from your parents. This is why people often look like their parents, and why you might look so different from your friends.

THE SHAPE OF DNA IS CALLED A DOUBLE HELIX.

NUCLEAR TRANSFER AND DOLLY THE SHEEP

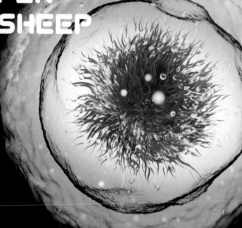

In the 1990's, scientists in Britain decided to clone a sheep. They wanted to make an animal that wasn't a mix of two parents, but rather an exact copy of another sheep. To do this, they did a nuclear transfer.

1: First, they took the nucleus out of the egg cell of a female sheep.

2: Then, they took a nucleus from the cell of a white-faced sheep and put it in the egg cell.

3: The egg cell was put in a black-faced sheep where it multiplied until it created a baby sheep. The black-faced sheep then gave birth to the lamb.

4: Soon enough, Dolly the cloned sheep was born. The scientists knew Dolly was a clone right away because she had a white face, just like the first sheep that gave a nucleus from one of its cells. Dolly looked nothing like the black-faced sheep that gave birth to her because Dolly did not share any DNA with the black-faced sheep.

Dolly was a clone of the first sheep because they both had the same DNA instructions in their cells. There was no mixing of DNA, so the cells just copied the first sheep.

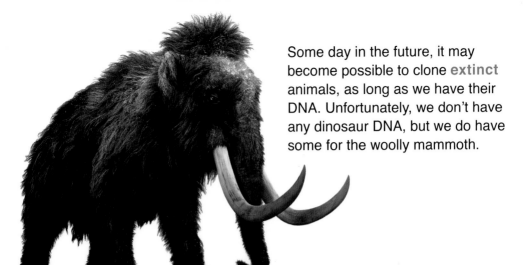

Some day in the future, it may become possible to clone **extinct** animals, as long as we have their DNA. Unfortunately, we don't have any dinosaur DNA, but we do have some for the woolly mammoth.

Lots of animals have been cloned since Dolly. We've made clones of everything from cats to camels. There are many good reasons to research cloning. In the future, we could create copies of animals with useful **traits**. For example, you could clone a fast horse to create lots of other fast horses.

NOTHING BUT STEM CELLS

In the future, we may not even need an egg cell to clone living things. Clones might be created in a laboratory, rather than in the body of another animal. Since Dolly, scientists have managed to create a mouse embryo by placing different stem cells together in a special gel. Nobody knows how to turn that embryo into a complete mouse yet – but don't worry, eventually some super-smart scientist will figure it out.

NANOTECHNOLOGY

HUMANS VS NATURE

But wait, with all the clever scientists and flashy new technology, can't we invent something even better than nature's replicator? Stem cells are great, but they can't make anything interesting like hamburgers, rocket engines, or double chocolate cake. If we are finally going to get our cake, we're going to need a different kind of replicator.

NANOTECHNOLOGY

Right now, scientists are working on something called nanotechnology. This is technology made up of really small machines and **particles**. Really, really, really small particles. A piece of nanotechnology will be around 1-100 nanometers in length. If you're wondering how small that is, there are one billion nanometers in a meter. A single hair is around 100,000 nanometers thick.

NANOPARTICLES

Nanotechnology is already being used in medicine. It is possible to send nanoparticles (particles that are less than 100 nanometers big) into the body that can grab onto certain cells that cause diseases – like **cancer** cells. Some nanoparticles carry drugs to kill these cells, while others explode when they are near to the diseased cells and destroy them. Because nanoparticles are so small, they only destroy the bad cells and do not damage any other parts of the body.

ATOMS

But scientists want to control things that are even smaller than cells. One day, far in the future, scientists want to control atoms. Atoms are the building blocks that make up all matter in the universe. They make everything, from the objects you can see to the air that you breathe. Even our cells are made up of different kinds of atoms that have been put together in a certain way.

ATOMS ARE TINY. MANY ATOMS ARE AROUND 0.1 NANOMETER WIDE.

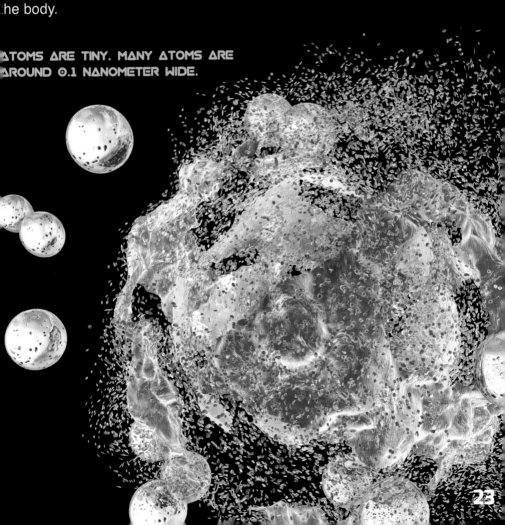

Atoms like to stick together. Some atoms stick together more easily than others, and this can make it difficult to break them apart. When atoms are linked together like this, they are called molecules, which are basically groups of different atoms. Pretty much everything you see around you is a collection of molecules made up of different atoms bonded together.

This might not sound like it has anything to do with replicators, but a lot of people think that nanotechnology will be really important in the future. One day, we may be able to rearrange atoms and create anything we want. How do you swap and change atoms, you ask? Well, you don't. You build a machine that will do it for you.

A SINGLE DROP OF WATER
IS MADE UP OF AROUND A
SEXTILLION MOLECULES. THAT IS
1,000,000,000,000,000,000,000
MOLECULES.

TINY, TINY ROBOTS

Sometime soon, we may build machines called nanorobots. These could be 3-D printed out of all sorts of materials, but they will probably be made out of a material like **silicon** (which a lot of small computer parts are made out of today). These machines will be so small that they can break molecules apart and put them back together again in a different combination. Remember, even our cells are made of atoms. This means that if a nanorobot had the ability to put atoms together to make any molecules it wanted, there is no limit on what it could create. It could make water, plastic, a toaster, or maybe even a human being.

MACHINES THAT MAKE MACHINES

If you think that sounds like a slow way of making things, you are right. It will take these tiny nanorobots a long time to make anything if they are doing it one molecule at a time! This is why the nanorobots would need to replicate themselves, so there would be lots of them all working together. After all, if they can make anything in the world, there is no reason they couldn't make more copies of themselves, right?

REPLICATORS: THE FUTURE

Are you surprised by how these replicators work? A lot of the replicators we've looked at aren't much like the ones in movies and books. The real replicators of the future will be tiny nanorobots, stem cells, and complicated 3-D printers. But even if they look different to the replicators in Star Trek, they are still doing the same thing, which is following a set of instructions to rearrange cells, atoms, or materials to create endless copies of anything we want.

While there are lots of interesting things we can currently do with all this technology, a lot of what we've talked about is still in the future. It might be 100 years before we get real nanorobots. But that doesn't mean it is impossible. We might just have to wait a little while.

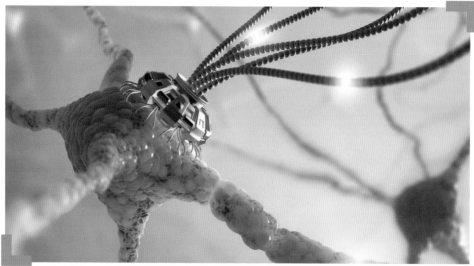

SOMETHING FROM NOTHING

The next step for replicators would be to create matter out of energy. If we could turn energy into matter, we wouldn't need ingredients like powders or cells – we wouldn't even need atoms, because we could create our own!

One of the easiest ways of doing this could be using photons. These are particles of light, which is a type of energy.

If you smash some photons together, you might create some electrons. If you don't understand how this works, don't worry – even scientists think this is complicated! All you need to know is that this is a way of turning energy into matter, which might mean we can create something from nothing in the future. But don't get too excited yet. It takes an incredible amount of energy to do this, and an atom is made up of all sorts of particles, not just electrons. For now, we will have to stick to 3-D printing.

THE DANGERS OF REPLICATING

GUNS

Creating things isn't all fun and games – when people are given the power to replicate things, you can bet that some people will use the power in dangerous ways. What if someone replicated something that wasn't safe, like a weapon? At this very moment, it is already possible to 3-D print a gun. And as the technology is becoming cheaper, soon almost anyone could be able to print guns in their backyard. What do you think? Should we stop people printing dangerous things like guns, or should people be able to print whatever they like?

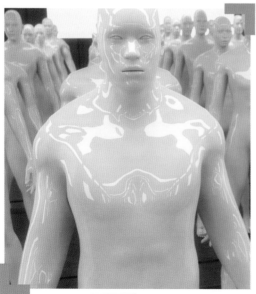

CLONING

As you may have noticed, nobody has tried to clone a human yet. Some people think that humans shouldn't be cloned, because we're not sure how safe it is. And what if future cloning technology fell into the wrong hands? Someone could clone themselves an army, creating as many super-soldiers as they wanted.

NANOTECHNOLOGY

What if those nanorobots are dangerous too? Some people are worried that we wouldn't be able to destroy the nanorobots if they went out of control, meaning there would be trillions upon trillions of tiny machines all around you, rearranging all the atoms! Others are worried that the material nanorobots are made from will be bad for the environment or bad for us if the nanorobots enter our bodies.

DON'T WORRY!

Well here's the good news. Scientists, governments, and lawmakers think very carefully about all this. Things like nanorobots and human cloning will be made very safe before they start testing them. Right now, we could use stem cells more than we do, but lots of governments want to make sure that using stem cells is safe for everybody first. Technology is amazing, but we need to be aware of the problems too.

WHY PRINT GUNS WHEN YOU CAN PRINT BURGERS?

WHAT WOULD YOU CREATE?

Just for a second, let's imagine that this is all possible right now. Let's imagine you don't need any special materials, cells, or atoms. Just by tapping a few buttons, your replicator machine would whir into life. The air would fizzle with electricity and suddenly any object you wanted would appear in front of you.

What would you make?
A brand new computer?
A TV the size of a house?
A rocket ship to go to the Moon?

A TRIPLE-CHOCOLATE-DOUBLE-FUDGE CAKE WITH EXTRA CHOCOLATE SPRINKLED ON TOP! IN FACT, LET'S HAVE TEN OF THEM. WE ARE USING REPLICATORS, AFTER ALL.

GLOSSARY

cancer	a serious disease caused by the uncontrolled dividing of cells
complex	complicated and consisting of many different parts
DNA	a type of acid that carries the genetic information in cells
donated	given away for a cause, such as charity
egg cell	the female reproductive cell in animals and plants
electrons	negatively charged particles that are found in all atoms
environment	the natural world
extinct	a species that is no longer alive
gel	a thick, jelly-like substance
genetic code	information that is passed from a parent to their offspring via genes
microscope	an instrument used by scientists to see very small things
nozzles	spouts that are fixed to the end of pipes or tubes that control the direction substances flow
nutrients	naturally occurring substances that cells need in order to multiply
organic	made of living matter
organs	(self-contained) parts of living things that have specific, important functions
particles	extremely small pieces of a substance
pregnant	when a mother develops a baby inside of her
recycle	to reuse materials for other purposes
replicate	make an exact copy of
scaffold	a temporary structure that keeps something in place
silicon	a chemical element
stem cells	cells that can multiply lots of times and turn into other types of cells
technology	machines or devices that are made using scientific knowledge
tissue	collections of cells that make up different parts of the body
traits	qualities or characteristics of a person or animal

INDEX